The Great
MATHEMACHICKEN
Hide and Go Beak

The Great MATHEMACHICKEN

Hide and Go Beak

NANCY KRULIK

Illustrated by CHARLIE ALDER

PIXEL✚INK

PIXEL+INK

Pixel+Ink is a division of TGM Development Corp.

Printed and bound in September 2021 at C&C Offset, Shenzhen, China.

Book design by Katrina Damkoehler

www.pixelandinkbooks.com

Library of Congress Cataloging-in-Publication Data
Names: Krulik, Nancy E., author. | Alder, Charlie, illustrator.
Title: Hide and go beak / Nancy Krulik ; illustrated by Charlie Alder.
Description: First edition. | [New York] : Pixel+Ink, 2021. |
Series: The great mathemachicken | Includes instructions for making
a simple machine. | Audience: Ages 5–8. | Audience: Grades 2–3. |
Summary: "A chicken hops a ride to school to see what the humans do
there all day and unlocks the superpowers of math and science,
which she uses to save the coop"—Provided by publisher.
Identifiers: LCCN 2021014205 (print) | LCCN 2021014206 (ebook) |
ISBN 9781645950325 (hardback) | ISBN 9781645950752 (ebook) |
Subjects: CYAC: Chickens—Fiction. |
Simple machines—Fiction. | Schools—Fiction.
Classification: LCC PZ7.K9416 Hi 2021 (print) | LCC PZ7.K9416 (ebook) |
DDC [Fic]—dc23
LC record available at https://lccn.loc.gov/2021014205
LC ebook record available at https://lccn.loc.gov/2021014206

Hardcover ISBN 978-1-64595-032-5
eBook ISBN 978-1-64595-075-2
First Edition
1 3 5 7 9 10 8 6 4 2

For my dad, Stephen Krulik,
math educator extraordinaire —N.K.

The author would like to thank Amanda
Burwasser for her assistance with this story.

For my own little Mathemachicken, W. —C.A.

Contents

1. Tag! You're It! 1

2. Sneaking Out 11

3. A Bird's-Eye View 17

4. *Egg*-citing *Eggs*-periments 25

5. Falling Feathers 34

6. Unlucky Clucky 39

7. A Zoober Idea 47

8. No One Likes an Angry Clucky . . . 53

9. *Whoosh! Bam! BOING!* 61

10. The Great Mathemachicken . . . 70

11. The Ants Dance 74

The Great
MATHEMACHICKEN
Hide and Go Beak

🐣 1 🐣

Tag!
You're It!

"Tag! You're it!" Clucky clucked.

He pecked his friend Chirpy's back.

Chirpy ruffled her wings.

But she didn't chase the other chicks.

"Chirpy's not playing," Shelly told Clucky.

"She's busy looking through the chicken wire," Buck-Buck added.

"Why do they call it *chicken* wire?" Shelly asked.

"It doesn't have a beak," Buck-Buck said.

"Or feathers," Squawky added.

"The *wire* keeps *chickens* stuck in the coop," Chirpy explained.

Chirpy didn't like being stuck in the coop.

She wanted to wander into the world outside the wire.

"We're not stuck," Clucky told Chirpy. "Watch."

The other chicks laughed at Clucky.

But not Chirpy.

She was too busy waiting for the boy and girl who lived in the house next to the coop.

Any minute now, Andy and Randy would come outside.

Like they did every morning.

And Chirpy would watch them.

Like *she* did every morning.

"Here they come!" Chirpy flapped her wings.

Andy and Randy ran into the yard.

Andy jumped onto the swing.

Randy pushed Andy's back.

Andy went higher.

And higher.

And higher still.

Until he looked like he was flying.

Chirpy wished she could go on the swing, so she could fly, too.

But the swing was *outside* the coop, and Chirpy was inside.

"OW!" Andy rubbed his head.

Clucky laughed. "What a cuckoo *cluck*!"

"We don't let acorns fall on *our* heads," Squawky said.

"That's because chickens are smarter than people," replied Shelly.

"No. It's because there are no trees over our coop," explained Chirpy. "So there are no acorns to fall on us."

"Nobody likes a smarty-pants," Clucky clucked at Chirpy.

"Chickens don't wear pants," Chirpy reminded him.

Clucky gave her a dirty look.

Buck-Buck pecked Squawky. "Tag! You're it!"

The chicks ran off to play.

But Chirpy stayed put and wondered:

Why did *things fall?*

"The bus is here!" Randy shouted.

Andy cheered. "Let's go! I can't wait to get to school!"

Chirpy wondered the same thing she wondered almost every morning:

What was school?

And why were Randy and Andy so egg-cited to go there?

(🥚 2 🥚)

Sneaking Out

"Here, chickie chickie."

The next morning, Randy and Andy's mom opened the gate.

She poured food into the feeder.

"Out of my way!" Clucky clucked. "I'm hungry."

Clucky was excited. "More food!"

Chirpy was excited, too.

But not about food.

Chirpy was excited because the gate was open.

And no one was watching.

Chirpy could go where no chicken had dared to go before. . . .

Out of the coop.

And into the world beyond the wire.

She would finally learn what was out there!

Chirpy snuck through the gate, hid among the yellow flowers, and waited.

Even though she was not sure what she was waiting for.

Honk! Honk!

Wow! What luck!

The bus was here.

Now, Chirpy had a way to get to school.

Whatever that was.

Randy and Andy got on the bus.

Chirpy got on, too.

Yay! Chirpy was off to school!

"Chirp chirp cha-ree!" she cheered.

"Here goes me!"

3

A Bird's-Eye View

"We have to hurry," Chirpy heard a boy say.

"I don't want to be late," added another.

He started running.

Everyone was running.

Feet were stomping all around Chirpy.

She had to keep from being stepped on.

"Chirp chirp cha-ree! Here goes me!"

Chirpy rolled into a room full of kids.

Which made her wonder:

At home kids stayed outside the coop.

Chickens stayed inside the coop.

Could school be a kid coop?

If someone saw Chirpy in a kid coop, would they make her leave?

Hmmm. . . .

Chirpy needed a hiding place, just like when the chicks played hide and go beak in the coop.

There, Chirpy usually hid flat on the ground and tried to blend in with the wood on the floor.

Sometimes that worked.

Sometimes it didn't. Chirpy looked at the ground in the classroom. Nope. Too many feet. How about hiding here?

Nope.

Or here?

Nope. Again.

Things seemed safer up on the ceiling. . . .

Chirpy flapped her wings.

But she didn't fly very high.

Chickens are not good fliers.

She would have to hop.

"Chirp chirp cha-ree! Here goes me!"

Chirpy had a bird's-eye view of

whatever happened next.

4

Egg-citing *Eggs*-periments

"What are we doing today, Mrs. Zoober?" a girl asked.

"We are building simple machines," the teacher answered. "We'll use our math and science skills."

One group of kids built a slide.

They rolled a ball down.

Whoosh!

INCLINED PLANE

"It works!" a girl cheered.

"Excellent!" Mrs. Zoober said. "What do we call the strong force that pulls the ball down the slide?"

"Gravity," the same girl answered. "It's what makes things fall."

Wow!

Chirpy had been in school for only a short time, but she had already learned why things fell.

A strong force called *gravity* pulled them down.

"Every machine needs a force to make it move," Mrs. Zoober told the kids.

That made Chirpy wonder:

What other things could she learn in school?

Chirpy moved close to another group.

RRRRINNNGGGG!

"Lunchtime!" The kids cheered.

They raced for the open door.

Chirpy didn't want to be left behind.

She hopped out of her hiding space,

and—

THUD.

Ow! Gravity *hurt*.

But it didn't stop Chirpy.

"Chirp chirp cha-ree!

Here goes me!"

5

Falling
Feathers

"Two. Four. Six."

A girl from Mrs. Zoober's class was counting her strawberries.

Chirpy knew what counting was.

Randy and Andy's mom counted the chickens in the coop.

But when *she* counted, she said, "One, two, three, four, five, six, seven, eight, nine, ten."

Chirpy looked down at the table.

She counted the berries.

One. Two. Three. Four. Five. Six.

Yep. The girl had the right number, even if her counting had sounded *peck*-uliar.

"I like skip counting," the girl told her friends, "because counting in groups of two makes math go faster."

That made Chirpy wonder:

What kind of things could a chicken skip count in groups of two?

Ants?

Eggs?

Feathers?

Two feathers.

Four feathers.

Six feathers.

Eight feathers.

Ten . . .

Whoops!

Chirpy stopped counting, but she was still *eggs*-ploding with excitement.

She couldn't wait to go back to the coop.

She wanted to show the other chicks what she had learned.

Besides, Chirpy was getting hungry.

And they didn't serve chicken feed in school.

6

Unlucky
Clucky

Uh-oh.

In the morning, Chirpy had snuck *out* of the coop.

But now the bus had brought her home, and she didn't know how to sneak back *in*.

It would be dark soon.

Dark outside the coop would be scary.

Chirpy wanted her mom.

She missed Buck-Buck, Shelly, and Squawky.

She even missed Cluck—

Whoops!

Wow. . . .

Someone had dug a tunnel under the wire.

What luck!

"Chirpy! There you are," her mother called.

"I was worried that you had slipped out of the coop with Clucky."

What! Clucky had gotten out of the coop, too?

Chirpy wondered where Clucky had gone, and what kinds of things *he* had learned today.

Clucky didn't usually want to learn anything.

"We thought the fox got you," said Shelly.

"What fox?" Chirpy asked.

"The one outside the coop!" Her mother ruffled her feathers.

"He was howling," explained Princess Lay-a, a friend of Chirpy's mother.

"And that's not the worst part," Buck-Buck added, her voice shaking.

"What is worse than a fox on the loose?" Chirpy wondered aloud.

"Clucky is still outside the coop," answered Squawky.

"He wanted to prove we were not stuck in here like you said," Shelly explained.

"So he dug a tunnel under the wire," Squawky added.

"And now he's out there alone!" Buck-Buck covered her face with her wings.

"Not alone," Princess Lay-a clucked. *"The fox is out there, too."*

7
A Zoober Idea

Ping!

An acorn fell from the tree outside the coop.

Chirpy watched it slide down the slide.

And roll to the seesaw.

That gave Chirpy a *Zoober* idea!

"We can save Clucky!" she chirped.

"Us?" Buck-Buck asked. "How?"

"We will catch the fox *before* he catches Clucky," Chirpy said.

Squawky shook his head. "We can't catch a fox," he squawked.

"He's bigger than we are," Shelly added.

"But there's only one fox," Chirpy replied, "and there are a lot of us."

Chirpy began counting chickens. "Two, four, six—"

"What kind of counting is that?" Princess Lay-a asked.

"Skip counting," Chirpy explained proudly. "It's faster. And we don't have a lot of time."

"Time for what?" Buck-Buck asked.
Chirpy leaped into action, using her
beak to draw out her plan.

"We are going to build a fox trap."

"How do you build a fox trap?" Squawky asked.

"We will need a slide. And a swing. Also string and—"

"Where are we going to find those things?" Princess Lay-a asked.

Chirpy pointed a wing at the yard.

"Out there."

"Y-y-you want us to leave the coop?" Shelly asked.

Chirpy nodded.

Buck-Buck took a step back. "B-b-but the fox is out there."

"That's why we have to build the trap *out there*," Chirpy explained.

She looked around the coop.

The other chickens were shaking.

"You can't *all* be scared," Chirpy said.

"Yes we can," Shelly answered. "Why
do you think they call us *chickens*?"
Nobody wanted to leave the coop.

But that wasn't going to stop Chirpy. "I'm going to catch that fox," she said. "Even if I have to do it by myself."

8

No One Likes
an Angry Clucky

"Clucky will be *eggs*-tra angry if we don't help," Buck-Buck told the others.

"No one likes an angry Clucky," Squawky agreed.

"Maybe we should listen to Chirpy," Shelly added.

One by one, the chickens snuck into
the yard.

"Now let's split into groups," Chirpy
ordered. "Each group will make part of
the trap."

Some chickens
rolled.

Others pushed.

A few pulled.

A couple even climbed.

Chirpy finished the whole thing off.

"All done," Chirpy cheered.

"What do we do now?" Buck-Buck asked.

Chirpy snuck behind a shrub. "We hide. And we wait."

9

Whoosh! Bam! BOING!

The chickens waited.

And waited.

And waited some more.

And then . . .

AROOOOO!

"That's the fox!" Squawky squawked.

Clucky came running into the yard.

The fox was close on his heels.

"HELP!" Clucky clucked. "He just bit my tail feather."

It was time to catch that fox!

"Go!" Chirpy shouted. "Now!"

Three chickens hopped onto the swing.

But the swing did not move.

It needed a force to get it started.

Uh-oh.

Without the swing, the trap would not work.

But . . .

A push was a force.

But how hard should the push be?

The chickens on the swing had to go way, way up.

That would take a lot of force.

"Push the swing!" Chirpy called out. *"Push as hard as you can!"*

The chicks swung high.

Higher.

Highest!

Whoosh!

"Chirp chirp cha-ree! Hooray for gravity!" Chirpy cheered.

"Hooray for *what*?" Buck-Buck asked.

There wasn't time to explain that gravity was the force that made the basket fall over the fox.

That fox wouldn't stay under the basket for long.

"Back to the coop!" Chirpy ordered.

The chickens hurried under the fence.

Clucky ran toward Chirpy.

She was sure he wanted to thank her.

But . . . no.

SLAM!

"Out of my way!" he clucked. "I'm going home!"

(₃10₃)

The Great Mathemachicken

Buck-Buck cheered, "Chirpy is a hero!"

"Yay, Super Chirpy!" Shelly joined in.

"Super Chirpy isn't much of a hero name," Buck-Buck said, shaking her head.

"Well, what kind of name should a hero have?" asked Squawky.

"One that shows she has superpowers," Buck-Buck replied.

Clucky laughed. "Chirpy doesn't
have superpowers."

"Yes she does," Buck-Buck said.

"She used them to save you," Shelly
added.

Princess Lay-a was curious. "What
kind of superpowers do you have?"

Chirpy thought.

"The powers of math and science," she finally said.

Shelly jumped up and down, excited. "That's it! Chirpy is

The Great Mathemachicken!"

"What about science?" Buck-Buck asked.

"The Great Math-Science-Chicken doesn't sound right," Shelly said after a moment.

"*The Great Math-e-ma-chick-en*," Chirpy repeated slowly. "I like that."

"I want a hero name," Clucky said.

"What makes you a hero?" Buck-Buck asked him.

Clucky crossed his wings. "The fox followed *me* to the trap."

"We can call you Super Fox Bait," Shelly suggested.

"Or not."

11

The Ants Dance

"Where are you going?" Chirpy's mother asked the next day.

"To school," Chirpy replied. "I am a superhero. I have a lot to learn."

"Even superheroes need breakfast," her mother clucked.

There was no time to wait for the feed, so Chirpy found an anthill.

She began catching her breakfast.

Two ants.

Four ants.

Six ants.

Eight.

The ants tickled Chirpy's beak.

It felt like they were doing an ant dance.

Honk! Honk!

The yellow bus pulled up.

Chirpy slid under the fence.

She ran for the bus.

"Chirp chirp cha-ree," she cheered. "Wait for me!"

An Egg-stra Special Whirly-Swirly Wheel-and-Axle Toy

Make your own simple machine!

You will need:

An empty coffee can

Construction paper

Cardboard

Markers or colored pencils

Scissors

Glue stick

30 inches of string

A grown-up to help you

Here's what you do:

1) Place the coffee can in the middle of a piece of construction paper and trace around it. Repeat this step on a second piece of construction paper.

2) Use your markers or colored pencils to draw designs inside each of the circles.

3) Ask your grown-up to help you cut out the circles.

4) Place the coffee can in the middle of a piece of cardboard and trace around it.

COFFEE

5) Ask your grown-up to cut out the cardboard circle.

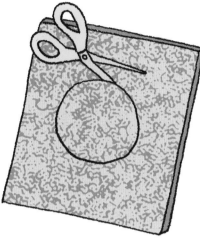

6) Glue one paper circle to each side of the cardboard circle. Make sure the colorful sides of the paper circles are facing up.

7) Ask your grown-up to poke two holes in the center of the disc. The holes should be about ½ inch apart.

8) Thread the ends of the string through the holes in your disc.

9) Tie the ends of the string together.

10) Move the disc to the center of the string.

11) Hold the ends of the string and flip the disc over and over like a jump rope. This will wind the string.

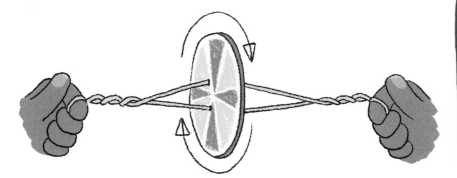

12) Once the string is wound tightly, pull hard on the ends. The pull is the force you need to make your circle whirl.

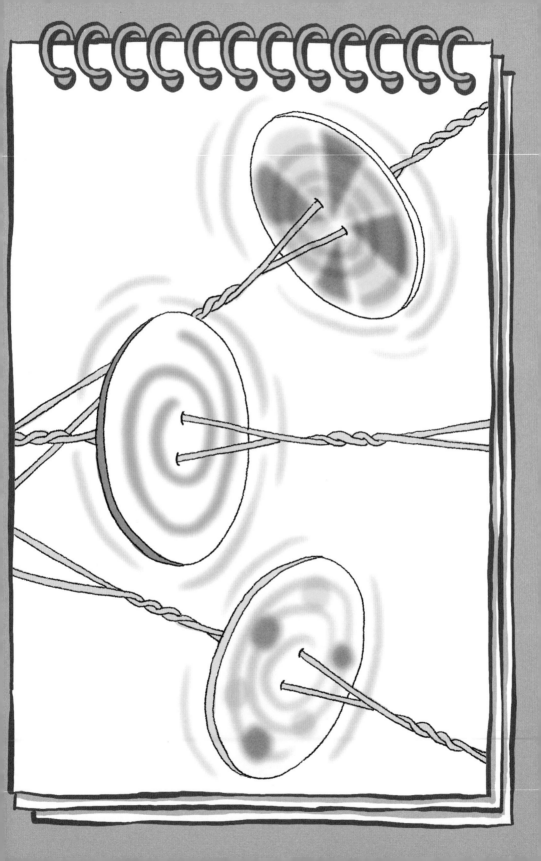

NANCY KRULIK is the international bestselling author of more than two hundred books for children. Her series, including Katie Kazoo, Switcheroo; George Brown, Class Clown; Magic Bone; Princess Pulverizer; and Ms. Frogbottom's Field Trips, are beloved around the world. She lives in New York City.

CHARLIE ALDER has written and illustrated many books for children, including *Daredevil Duck* and *Chicken Break!* When not drawing chickens, Charlie can be found in her studio drinking coffee, arranging her crayons, and inventing more accidental animal heroes. She lives in Devon, England.